-the-
PIRATE
KIDS

WITHDRAWN

Pirate Fest!

Calico Kid

BY Johanna Gohmann
ILLUSTRATED BY Addy Rivera Sonda

An Imprint of Magic Wagon
abdobooks.com

With love to David. Thank you for letting me sit at home and write pirate books. —JG

To the young readers who are shaping a kinder world. —ARS

abdobooks.com

THIS BOOK CONTAINS
RECYCLED MATERIALS

Written by Johanna Gohmann
Illustrated by Addy Rivera Sonda
Edited by Tyler Gieseke
Art Directed by Candice Keimig
Designed by Victoria Bates

Library of Congress Control Number: 2019956814

Publisher's Cataloging-in-Publication Data

Names: Gohmann, Johanna, author. | Rivera Sonda, Addy, illustrator.
Title: Pirate fest! / by Johanna Gohmann ; illustrated by Rivera Sonda, Addy.
Description: Minneapolis, Minnesota : Magic Wagon, 2022. | Series: The pirate kids
Summary: Piper and Percy are prepared for Pirate Fest, the annual competition for young pirates to show off their skills. Percy desperately wants to win and be named Perfect Pirate, but one of the contestants keeps giving him a hard time.
Identifiers: ISBN 9781532138171 (lib. bdg.) | ISBN 9781644944769 (pbk.) | ISBN 9781532138898 (ebook) | ISBN 9781532139253 (Read-to-me ebook)
Subjects: LCSH: Competitions--Juvenile fiction. | Friendship--Juvenile fiction. | Pirates--Juvenile fiction. | Bullying--Juvenile fiction. | Adventure and adventurers--Juvenile fiction.
Classification: DDC [E]--dc23

Table of Contents

Chapter #1
Who Will Win?

Percy bounces excitedly around the deck of the family ship, jabbing at the air with his wooden sword. The family is headed to Pirate Fest—an annual contest where young pirates compete to show off their pirate skills.

Suddenly, Percy's shiny new boots catch on a nail, and he trips.

"Blimey, brother!" Piper laughs. "Careful!"

He stands and dusts himself off. "I'm just excited! I can't wait to win the Perfect Pirate award!"

"Oh yeah?" Piper teases. "Maybe I'll take the top prize!"

Percy rolls his eyes. He pulls a piece of pancake from his pocket and feeds it to their parrot, Poppy. "I've been practicing all year for Pirate Fest! I'm going to win!"

Their father comes up behind them. He wears a velvet pirate hat that he saves for special occasions. He pats Percy on the head. "Remember, lad, the main thing is to have fun!"

"Oh, I plan to have loads of fun." Percy grins. "And win."

"Land ho!" Piper suddenly shouts.
"We made it!"

The ship sails toward a small island. A scarlet banner stretches between two coconut trees. It reads: Welcome to Pirate Fest!

"Land ho!" Poppy squawks.

9

Chapter #2
The Big Day Begins

Piper and Percy disembark with their parents and hurry toward a large wooden stage. There are swarms of other pirate children, and everyone is chattering with excitement.

A tall man in a golden coat strides onto the stage.

"Welcome to Pirate Fest! I'm Captain Goldie Gibbs!"

He smiles, and a spotlight flashes off his teeth. All of the top ones are made of solid gold!

"Are ye ready for some fun?" He claps his hands, and everyone cheers.

"Yo ho ho! Then let's get to it! And at the end o' the day, we'll see who takes home the top prize!" Captain Gibbs gestures behind him to a small treasure chest.

Percy strains to stand on his tippy toes and get a better look. But suddenly someone steps down hard on his foot.

"Ouch!" Percy yelps.

He turns to see a boy with a long red feather poking out of the top of his pirate hat.

"Sorry," the boy says, but he smiles meanly. Percy doesn't think he looks very sorry at all.

"Alright, little buccaneers!" Captain Gibbs booms. "Away to the competitions!"

The other children happily scatter, but Percy looks down at his new boots. He sees a big dusty mark where the boy stomped on him.

"You OK, Perce?" Piper asks.

"Yeah," he sighs. "Come on! Let's do the peg leg race first!"

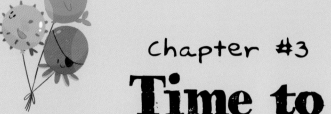

Chapter 3

Time to Walk the Plank

The children have a great time, and Piper and Percy both do well at the competitions.

Now it's time for the final contest, plank walking, where each child must walk across a long wooden plank without falling into the tank below. The tank is filled with blue foam balls that look like the sea.

Piper makes it the whole way across, and the crowd cheers wildly for her. Now it's Percy's turn . . .

"Let's go, Percy! You can do it!" Piper cheers him on.

Percy nervously steps onto the plank, and he is happy he wore his new pirate boots, which make him feel steady on his feet. He carefully starts across, and the crowd goes quiet. He creeps along and is almost to the other side when someone suddenly shouts, "Don't fall, ye landlubber!"

The noise makes Percy jump.
"Whoa!" he shouts. He slips off the
plank and crashes into the blue foam
below.

"Aww . . ." the crowd groans.

"Argh, ye almost made it, matey!"
Captain Gibbs calls.

Percy crawls out of the tank, a look
of defeat on his face. Piper hurries to
help him.

"Aye, brother, you did a great job!"
Piper says. "That scallywag with
the red feather made you lose your
balance!"

"Wait, it was him?" Percy scans the crowd, and again he sees the boy with the long red feather. The boy gives him another mean grin. Percy starts toward him, but suddenly his mother and father hurry over.

"Come!" their mother says. "They're about to name the Perfect Pirate!"

Chapter #4
A Moment to Treasure

"Argh, it's been a magnificent day, and I hope ye all had loads o' fun!" Captain Gibbs shouts from the stage. "Now, the moment ye all have been waiting for!"

Piper grabs Percy's hand in excitement.

"This year's Perfect Pirate award goes to . . ."

Percy squeezes Piper's hand tightly.

". . . Piper Calico!"

The crowd erupts in cheers. Percy tries to hide his disappointment, and he claps loudly for his sister. "Way to go, Pipe!"

Piper shyly climbs onstage, and Captain Gibbs gestures toward the chest she won. She happily lifts the lid. Suddenly, her face falls.

"Blow me down!" Captain Gibbs shouts. "Someone stole the treasure!"

The crowd gasps, and Percy races onstage.

"Hey! That's not fair!" he shouts. "No one can take my sister's prize!"

He peers into the chest. Sure enough, it's empty! Except for one tiny thing that immediately catches Percy's eye.

"Wait!" Percy says. "I know who took it!" He reaches in and plucks out a red feather.

Percy scans the crowd, and then he sees him—the boy with the mean grin . . . who is now trying to sneak away!

"Him!" Percy points. "He's the thief!"

The boy freezes, and several gold coins tumble out of his cloak.

"Stop right there!" Captain Gibbs commands. "Please bring the treasure back to its rightful owner . . . Miss Piper Calico!" Embarrassed, the boy shuffles back to the stage.

"Actually, Captain," Piper says, "I think my brother, Percy, also deserves some of the booty. For only a truly Perfect Pirate knows how to find missing treasure!"

31

Captain Gibbs smiles. "Very true, lassie!" He claps his hand on Percy's back. "It looks like this year we have two Perfect Pirates!"

Percy grins at his sister as the crowd cheers. Together, they take a bow.